*To my parents for teaching me to appreciate animals in their natural habitats.*

Brimming with creative inspiration, how-to projects, and useful information to enrich your everyday life, Quarto Knows is a favourite destination for those pursuing their interests and passions. Visit our site and dig deeper with our books into your area of interest: Quarto Creates, Quarto Cooks, Quarto Homes, Quarto Lives, Quarto Drives, Quarto Explores, Quarto Gifts, or Quarto Kids.

Text and illustrations © 2016 Kirsten Sims. *Balthazar the Great* © 2016 Orfeu Negro

First Published in Portugal as *Balthazar, O Grande* in 2016 by Orfeu Negro,
Rua Silva Carvalho, n.º 152 - 2.º, 1250 - 257 Lisboa | Portugal

First published in the English language in 2017 by Lincoln Children's Books, an imprint of The Quarto Group.
The Old Brewery, 6 Blundell Street, London N7 9BH, United Kingdom.
T (0)20 7700 6700  F (0)20 7700 8066  **www.QuartoKnows.com**

This paperback edition published 2018

The right of Kirsten Sims to be identified as the author/illustrator of this work has been asserted by her in accordance with the Copyright, Designs and Patents Act, 1988 (United Kingdom).

A catalogue record for this book is available from the British Library.

978-1-78603-126-6

The illustrations were created using gouache and ink
This book was hand lettered by the artist

Manufactured in Guangdong, China RD0618

9 8 7 6 5 4 3 2 1

MIX
Paper from responsible sources
FSC® C101537
www.fsc.org

# BALTHAZAR
# THE GREAT

Kirsten Sims

LINCOLN
Children's Books

Balthazar was *the world's* GREATEST violin-playing polar bear!

Well, he used to be **the greatest.**

These days he was the only violin-playing polar bear
left in all the world's circuses. He missed his home, but most of all
he missed his grandpa, who had given him his first violin.

One night,
Balthazar was
set free!

He could go home at last.
As long as he could figure out where that was...

"Home must be around here somewhere," he thought.

But some where was a very big place.

Balthazar said GOODBYE to old friends.

And tried to make new ones.

He met others who were looking for home, too.

Some days were happy days.

But sometimes Balthazar felt more *LOST* and lonely than ever.

He was beginning to think his journey would never end.

But just as he was about to turn back...

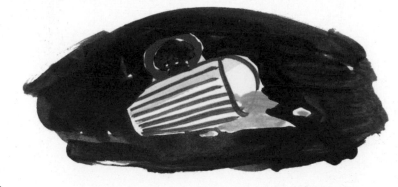

...he saw a familiar face.

Could it REALLY be...?

GRANDPA BALTHAZAR!

Balthazar was finally HOME!

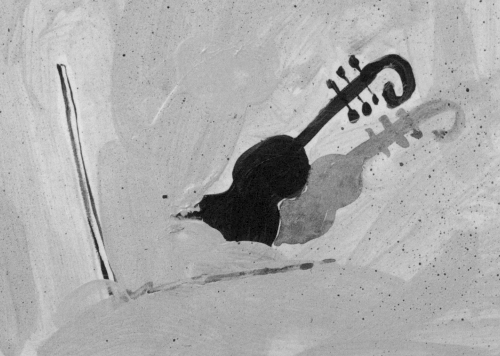

And he felt GREATER than ever.